Certified

and

Seven Things

AMY LAURENS

OTHER WORKS

Find other works by the author at
www.amylaurens.com

Certified

and

Seven Things

INKLET #27

AMY LAURENS

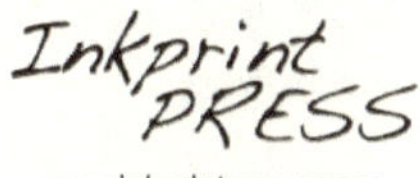

www.inkprintpress.com

Print ISBN: 978-1-925825-25-1
eBook ISBN: 9781393202561

www.inkprintpress.com

National Library of Australia Cataloguing-in-Publication Data
Laurens, Amy 1985 –
Certified and Seven Things (Double Issue)
48 p.
ISBN: 978-1-925825-25-1
Inkprint Press, Canberra, Australia
1. Young Adult Fiction—Fantasy—Dark Fantasy 2.
Young Adult Fiction—Short Stories 3. Young Adult
Fiction—Coming Of Age

First Print Edition: February 2020
Cover image © Мария Ткачук via Pixabay
Cover design © Inkprint Press
Interior art © Amy Laurens

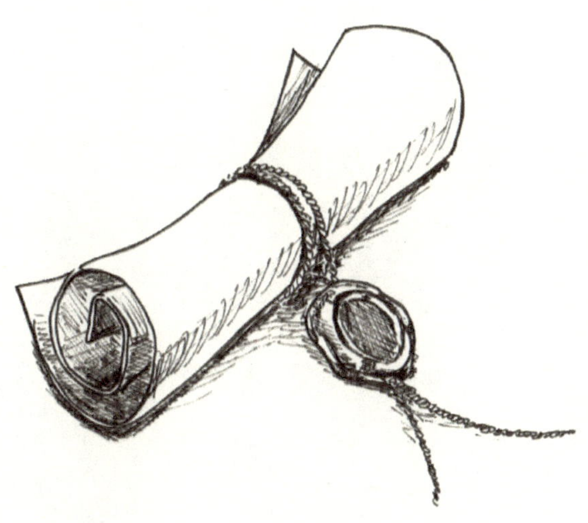

CERTIFIED

My name's Anna and I'm certified to bring people back from the dead. Sometimes they don't want to come, but that's neither here nor there.

What matters is that I'm certified. Licensed. Allowed. And I'm the youngest person ever to qualify as a Raiser; but that doesn't matter either. I'm qualified. And being qualified means I have to follow the rules.

That's why, when Millicent asked me to Raise her boyfriend Victor, I said no. I'm not allowed to Raise people I know. We're only allowed to Raise people that have been tagged for us.

The authorities do the tagging; no one knows what they do with the people once they're Raised. You hear stories, but everyone agrees it's to help the war effort. So I guess it doesn't matter what they're doing.

All that matters is that we can't Raise people who aren't tagged. The authorities think that if we could Raise anyone willy-nilly, it would lead to self-indulgence, Raising everyone we ever loved who died.

I don't think so. Some people are better off dead, and I like to think I'm mature enough to realise that. If they were supposed to be alive, the authorities would have tagged them.

That didn't convince Millicent, though. "You bitch," she said. "You'd bring him back if he was your boy-friend."

"I wouldn't," I said, jutting out my chin.

"You would too, and you know it."

I didn't know it. Rules are important. I don't break rules. Especially when I'm the youngest Raiser ever, and I need to keep my job. Mum would've killed me if I wasn't earning.

"You bring him back, or else." Millicent leaned over me, trying to look threatening. She just looked fat.

"He hasn't been tagged," I said. "No one wants him."

She leered. "*I* want him. I love him."

I snorted. "You love him? Big, mature Millicent is in *wuv*? Yeah, right." She had the heart of an ice queen, use and abuse.

"Yeah," she said. "Right." She leaned closer and I could see the blackheads on her nose.

I tried not to laugh.

"Bring him back," she said. "Or. Else."

"Go screw yourself," I said. "Some-one has to, now Victor's gone."

Her nose trembled and red spots appeared on her cheeks.

I rolled my eyes. She always was melodramatic. What she failed to realise was that anger didn't suit her; it made her look like a cow having an apoplectic fit.

I opened my mouth to tell her so, but she stormed out. Good riddance. My work was more important than false friends. Besides, I figured she'd get over it.

I figured wrong.

Three days later, I stared down at the face of my own boyfriend as he lay on the slab. I thought he'd gone to his Aunt's.

Millicent had sent me a letter, gloating.

Do you like your birthday present? I think the dried blood really suits his complexion.

It's been nearly three days, and he hasn't been tagged. No one wants him; you Raise him or no one does. I know you'll do it. And when you're done, I'll bring Victor over.

If you don't… Well, I know where your family lives.

I stared at Aaron, lying there on the morgue table. I didn't *want* to break the rules. I've never broken rules. Mum always said I was a good girl, that I did what I was supposed to, and I wanted to believe that.

But it was Aaron.

I'd loved him since the day I'd met him—nine weeks, three days, four hours and thirty-six seconds, now. Thirty-eight.

And he loved me too. He told me so. We leant up against the bricks of the school building after hours and he put his hand up my shirt and told me. "I love you so much I can't breathe," he said once.

I loved him. So I Raised him.

Sure, some people are better off dead.

But he wasn't one of them. Sometimes the authorities make mistakes. I'm mature. I can tell.

The authorities came to visit not long after. It wasn't *so* bad. They let Aaron go. And they made it nice and quick for me. And clean. And they let me keep my certificate.

My name's Anna and I'm certified to bring people back from the dead. But I won't any more. The dead can't raise the dead.

THE MAKING OF
CERTIFIED

This is an old story now, written back in my accidental period of punishing naivety with death. I was in university, probably in my post graduate studies, and writing short stories was a relatively new thing for me. It seems to have worked in this instance, though, as this was one of the first short stories I ever sold.

And although the point of the story is kind of to mock teen romances, and teens who are overly serious about teen romances, let's be clear here: I met my husband when I was sixteen, and married him at twenty. And so far, that's working out really well for me ;)

SEVEN THINGS

THE FIRST THING IS THE MOONLIGHT, bright and startling to the eye.

The second is the frame of the deck, old hardwood washed white, entwined by creeping leaves.

The third thing is the table, long, covered by a mostly-white cloth, with silverware and white porcelain crockery and glasses strewn about. The carcasses of fruit mingle with used napkins, the juice of plums and cherries blotted like blood on the cloths. In the moonlight, it looks like a perfect scene, the aftermath of revelries; but the fourth thing is that some of the plates are broken, and some of the glasses chipped. The food has not been cleared, the serving dishes not stacked. This table has been left in a hurry.

The fifth thing is this: in the centre of the table, framed by moonlight that's framed by the deck, is something that catches the light and throws it out again, dazzling the eye—and the mind.

It is glass, or crystal maybe, the kind that resonates with a deep, echoing note somewhere in the chest. It's all edges and planes, sculpted, some sides rough and natural, some silky smooth. It's twined around with the same plant that frills the deck posts, which, looking closer, is covered with tiny, white stars.

Their fragrance underlies the sharp, sweet smell of fruit—something warm and spicy, summer in a flower. It might even be jasmine, in much the same way that a lion might even be a cat.

Looking closer still, it seems the flowers are not merely reflecting the light, though there is plenty of it. No, they glow from deep within their silvered throats, some pulsing softly, some dim and fading.

And now, the sixth thing: the crystal, which stands as tall as a man's forearm on a platform of moulded, polished silver, is pulsing too, breathing *something* in, and exhaling light. Perhaps it is the moon's own rays the crystal imbibes, transforming it into a light softer and more silver.

But the flowers are fading, wilting, and upon reflection the tableware is not randomly strewn about after all. It is scattered, interrupted, to be sure— but the interruption is not random. The glasses all lean outwards and only the plates nearest the crystal are shattered, like some strange explosion has occurred, for though chairs and places remain, the floor under the table where the crystal sits has been swept clean, and dust has gathered in rings concentric from the middle of the table.

This, then, is the seventh thing: the dust, lots of it. More than there should be for a party this fine, in a house this grand. Surely the deck would have been swept beforehand; the guests could not have trod this much dirt up from the yard. And dust is not really dirt, anyway. Dust is mostly skin, they say: dead skin, dry skin, old cells sloughed off and cast away.

There is a lot of dust. Enough for all the guests.

The last of the flowers pulses, withers, breaks free from its sepal and falls, drifting down to the table. The crystal breathes in, and this time, there is no exhale.

THE MAKING OF
SEVEN THINGS

Wow. I'd quite forgotten when I wrote this story, and hunting down the time frame led me down quite the rabbit hole. As it turns out, I wrote this story in November of 2014, when I was pregnant with my daughter. 2014 had been a rough year in some ways (though nowhere near as bad as the impending 2016 would be): it was the first time I ever lived away from the city where I was born.

I know. I know. I'm the kind of person who, when people say, "Oh, do you live around here?", can reply with "Born and bred!" I used to be more sensitive about this fact, but life's too short for being ashamed of knowing where you want to live, ha.

But! The story! This was back in the relatively early days of the Darkness and Good blog, a now-defunct blog that Liana Brooks and I ran (with the later addition of Thea van Diepen) with the tagline "mostly-unedited, mostly-weekly stories". We started the blog in January of 2014 after I'd read *The Curiosities*, a collection of short stories by Maggie Stiefvater, Brenna Yovanoff and Tessa Gratton which they had compiled from *their* short story blog, the Merry Sisters of Fate.

I'd been struggling to get back into writing since my son had been born. A weekly short-story challenge sounded perfect.

I don't remember the inspiration behind this story in particular, which makes me think that there wasn't one: I've said before that some stories just appear out of the ether, and I suspect this was one of those: I had a deadline, I needed a story for the blog, I sat down and literally wrote the first thing I could 'see'.

The first thing is the moonlight, bright and startling to the eye.

The story, such as it is, simply unspooled from there.

DOWNLOAD YOUR FREE EBOOK

When you buy a print book from Inkprint Press, we like to say THANK YOU by offering you the ebook for free!

Please head to
www.inkprintpress.com/inklets/27/
and the use the coupon INKLET27 to get your copy of this Inklet in epub AND mobi today!
(Coupon will only work once.)

HOW NOT TO ACQUIRE A CASTLE

CHAPTER ONE

ON A HARD PLASTIC CHAIR IN THE FRONT row of the Great Hall in the world's fifth-best evil overlording academy, with its red-wooden parquetry floor that spoke of wealth and the beige, square panels of sound-boards speaking of conservatism on the walls, Mercury sat, pointedly not sweating.

Partly, this was because the Academy Administrators had deigned to turn on the air-conditioning earlier in the day, in recognition of the fact that the hall would be packed out with approximately six hundred bodies, all here to celebrate the graduation of about a third of that crowd.

But mostly, Mercury was pointedly not sweating because she made it a point never to sweat, sweat being an indication that she was working hard, and hard work being antithetical to her way of life.

However. If she *had* been sweating right now, it would not have been due to the uncomfortable warmth of six hundred packed bodies that even the air-conditioning system couldn't completely shift, or, in fact, from overexertion. Instead, it would have been caused by an even more unfamiliar concept in Mercury's emotional vocabulary: nervousness.

Mercury did not *get* nervous. Mercury got things *done*.

So the fact that she was sitting here, in the front row of the Great Hall, about to graduate from Evil Overlording Academy (with distinction), and was feeling *nervous*... She crumpled the black paper program in her pale fists. It made her furious, that's what it did.

Abjectly furious, that snooty-tooty Deviran with his stupid morals and his stupid I-don't-want-to-be-here and his stupid Overlords-are-empty-figureheads and his stupid face sitting ten people over, looking implacable with his deep brown skin and barely-there, precision-groomed beard, as though he knew it gave him a stupid air of alluringly stupid mystery...

Mercury scowled and searched for the train of thought that had been derailed, yet again, by Deviran's stupidity.

Ah. Yes. She was angry because she was nervous because she wasn't absolutely entirely one hundred and fifty percent sure that she'd beaten Deviran in their final exams, and 1) being anything less than a hundred and fifty percent certain of anything made her cranky, and 2) being beaten by Deviran for dux of the year would be utterly unbearable. She flicked away a piece of fluff that had become snagged under her immaculately magenta-painted nails and smoothed out the black paper program.

In the front corner of the hall, the starkly-attired string quartet with their traditional black instruments began playing the March of the Oncoming Doom. The screechy scrapes of hundreds of chairs on the hall's wooden floor sounded as the crowd climbed to its collective feet.

Mercury sat with her arms firmly folded for a few moments longer, until her best friend Sparky kicked her in the ankle.

"Get up, idiot," Sparky hissed, hints of real flame flickering through her flame-coloured pixie cut.

"No," Mercury said, flouncing to her feet and tossing her own glossy brown hair back over her shoulders. Four years she'd been playing by the Academy's rules in order to get what she wanted, and she'd had just about enough. Other people's rules should only be applied to plebs too stupid to invent their own.

Sparky rolled her eyes somewhere over Mercury's head before focusing on the stage, where the ceremonial party had begun entering.

Mercury clenched her jaw and narrowed her own eyes as the teachers of the Evil Overlording Academy filed onto the stage, dressed in their formal finery. Each teacher had their own distinctive look that matched their personality and their Overlording style, from severe charcoal suits to jet-black leathers, pastel ball-gowns and gem-toned lingerie and eye-blinding spandex, and even on one tiny old woman at the back, worn jeans and a grey flannel shirt. She was the one to watch out for, of course; Mercury could respect an Overlord who was confident enough in their abilities that they didn't need to telegraph them. It wasn't a look *she* would consider, of course, but still. She could respect it.

The band's march finished and, after a moderately awkward pause, the crowd sat. The Principal, pale skin and dark hair matching his suspiciously vampiric red-and-black suit, took the podium, and Mercury narrowed her eyes. He was doing a superb job of hiding his emotions—he was a premier Evil Overlord, after all—but she was Mercury, and unlike anyone else, she had the benefit of being able to rummage through people's consciousnesses. She was better at adding things *into* people's minds than taking information out, but he was telegraphing fear loudly enough that she could sense it without trying overly much.

Mercury pursed her lips.

Hmm.

The Principal cleared his throat at the blackened-wood podium, and the fear made it into his usually-unreadable eyes. "Before we begin," he said, and Mercury's stomach did a peculiar kind of flip-flop. "I have a pressing announcement to make regarding the safety of our students and their families."

He cleared his throat again and took out a sheet of paper from his pocket, unfolding it carefully and smoothing out the creases before beginning again. "The Council"—quiet booing echoed around the hall, and Mercury tsked impatiently— "have asked me to recommend that students from Tumul Tuos seriously consider postponing their return to town for a few days. The city is dealing with a *situation* at present which may present a danger to our students' health and safety."

Mercury's hands fisted at her sides and she forced herself to remain seated. What was wrong with her city? What had the Council mucked up now? A risk to the students' safety? There had to be more he wasn't telling them. Gently, Mercury tugged on his consciousness, implanting the suggestion that it might be better to share the news than to keep it secret. After all, how could they fight an enemy they didn't know?

"There are, ah..." He trailed off, glancing side to side as though wondering why his mouth had decided to continue.

Mercury didn't snicker, but she did press her lips together in satisfaction.

The Principal took a deep, steadying breath and seemed to change tack. "There has been one death already. The family have already been notified, so it is with much regret that I must inform you that Woovermyer will no longer be with us at the Evil Overlording Academy."

Murmurs broke out around the room, not all of them sad—to be expected in a school devoted to raising the next generation of dictators (ish) and despots (of sorts).

Mercury, however, crushed her pro-gram in her left hand, fist so tight her nails bit her palm.

"You okay?" Sparky murmured, leaning towards her.

Mercury gave a single, tense shake of her head and stared at the podium. Dead. Livie Woovermyer was dead in *her city*. And the Council hadn't done anything to stop it. Couldn't do anything to stop it, probably, given they'd warned the students to stay away. Livie hadn't been the strongest candidate in the year level, but she was no lightweight, either. It would take a lot of power to kill a Seven.

Enough was enough. A good thing Mercury was about to graduate at the top of the class, giving her the right to knock the lowest ranking current Overlord off their perch. Tumul Tuos would be hers in a matter of hours. And then there'd be no more of these wasteful deaths. Her city would be safe at last.

Madame Pompadour was up the front now, elbow gloves the same glimmery silver colour as her elaborate, piled-curls wig, eyelids gleaming with matching silver eye shadow, and abruptly Mercury realised Madame was there to make the announcement that would change her life forever. She leaned forward in her seat, ready to stand when her name was called.

"And now the announcement you've all been dying for," the Political Alliances teacher trilled, the frills on her evening gown fluttering as she moved. "The dux of this year's cohort!"

Sweat slicked Mercury's palms. Irritated, she reached over and wiped them on Sparky's thigh.

Sparky pushed Mercury's hands back into her own personal space bubble and Mercury, nervous to the edge of distraction, let her.

"Will you please join me in welcoming to the stage, our wonderful dux for this year, Deviran Goodsmith!"

Mercury froze halfway to standing. "Did she just say Deviran?" she whispered furiously to Sparky.

Sparky hauled her forcibly back down into her seat. "Yes," she hissed back. "Sit down, you're making a fool of yourself."

Mercury's spine snapped upright as she sat, and she arranged the folds of her long black skirt demurely. "No I'm not." She closed her eyes. "Deviran's going up to the stage, isn't he?" Even at a whisper, the misery in her voice was clear, but this time, she didn't care.

Sparky reached over and squeezed her hand.

Mercury squeezed back, lacing her fingers through Sparky's, and held tight as all her plans and dreams vanished in front of her.

A stone had landed in her chest. That must be it. Some strange sort of magic that made her chest contract and sink, and made the world distort for just a moment, long enough to trick her into thinking Deviran had beaten her so that someone could jump in front of her and yell SURPRISE!

Any moment now.

Any moment.

She refused to open her eyes and watch Deviran parading across the stupid stage like some stupid stupid-person, receiving his stupid medal and stupid symbolic crest pin.

It was that last exam question. She'd known Deviran would pull out his ridiculous 'Evil Overlords are merely figureheads, the Business Guild is where the power really lies' rant that everyone had heard a million times back when he was younger and angrier, and she'd tried to counter it, she really had.

She'd argued for the importance of the Overlording position, for the power of having a symbolic figure to unite the population in their hatred, for having a person able to make all the difficult, necessary decisions the Council was too weak and spineless to make... But it hadn't been enough. Everything she'd worked for, everything she'd set out to prove—and it wasn't enough.

There were words, there were names, and then forever later, once she'd died twice already, Sparky elbowed her in the ribs. "Come on," Sparky muttered. "We're up next."

And sure enough, there was a shuffling of presenters as the last of the Powers Behind The Thone graduates departed the stage, and the next speaker announced in threatening, funereal tones, "The Over-lording cohort."

Mercury blinked furiously and followed Sparky to the end of the line at the right side of the stage. The other candidates proceeded one at a time across the stage, two girls and then stupid Deviran, and then a handful more and then Sparky, and then the speaker was calling her name.

Hands fisted, Mercury tossed her head high, climbed the four steps, and marched across the stage. She wouldn't look at them, the stupid faculty who'd denied her the city she rightfully deserved, and she wouldn't look the other way either, at the classmates and crowd undoubtedly snig-gering at her failure.

She shook hands with the presenter, and while he pinned the tiny crossed-swords badge on her collar, her eyes betrayed her and slid towards the aud-ience. Her stomach flipped as she saw the crowd of parents and friends behind the rows of students, all the way to the back of the hall, twenty rows at least, illuminated by the late afternoon light streaming in through the ceiling-high windows to the right. Everyone had someone here to watch them graduate. Everyone except Weird Al—and her.

The presenter finished with her pin, muttered something to her, and offered his hand again. Mercury coldly ignored it and strode from the stage. It didn't matter. None of it mattered. Tumul Tuos was her city anyway, and no one could change that. She'd think of something. She'd take a day or two out, make some plans…

And she could always hope that Deviran would choose some other Overlording territory. He'd be stupid to, but then again, he was stupid, so. Mercury could hope.

All at once, mid-way down the steps off the stage, Mercury came to rigid attention, scanning the room. Somewhere out there in the crowd, an exchange of power had just taken place, and it felt… unusual.

But the final few students were backing up behind her and muttering, so Mercury headed back toward her seat, craning her head all the while and searching for some sign of whatever it was that had just discharged a dizzyingly quiet amount of power into the room.

She sat, and Sparky leaned over. "Okay?"

"Mm," said Mercury. "Did you feel…" She accidentally caught the eye of the student behind her and twisted back to face the front.

"Feel what?"

Mercury turned it over in her mind. It had felt like a large shot of power discharged very quietly—but perhaps it hadn't been. Perhaps it had only been a small discharge after all, something most people wouldn't have noticed.

But still, something about it had tugged on her. It very nearly felt like something she'd felt before, only she *knew* she'd never sensed that kind of discharge before.

She shook her head. "Never mind. Don't worry."

Sparky sighed and straightened. "It's fine, Mercury," she said, drily exasperated.

"I know you didn't win, but I promise, you'll live through it."

Mercury waved a hand for silence.

The power had just discharged again, and it had come from somewhere in the back corner, far away from the windows and light.

Impatiently, Mercury waited for the formalities to conclude. The crowd stood while the quartet played the exit march, and the stage party left, Mercury tapping her foot all the while.

The moment the last notes of the march died away, Mercury turned and headed to the back corner, weaving in and out of the students and parents who had seemed to explode slowly but inexorably out from the neat rows of seating, ignoring Sparky's calls behind her. Power, something that tugged in a way that was strange and familiar, all at once. She pushed her way through a family posing for pictures—and halted.

In the shadows of the back corner, Deviran stood with his family, with his stupid, smug little smile, looking as tall and dark and stupidly alluring as ever. Prat.

His mother, short but sleek, and his father—tall, and utterly terrifying in a way not at all diminished by his gleaming smile—gushed over him, patting his back and hugging him tight. Within moments the Principal was there, glibly shaking hands and congratulating them on the success of their son. Something flickered across his consciousness, and also Deviran's father's—some moment of recognition in response to what they were saying.

But Mercury brushed it aside just as the mother brushed melodramatic tears from her cheeks and handed Deviran a silver-wrapped package about as long as her hand but half the width.

That. That was the source of the strange, magical feeling. Mercury watched hawk-eyed as Deviran un-wrapped the gift. A glimpse of gold set her pulse racing—What was it? What did it do? Could she steal it?—and then the paper fell away to the floor, and Deviran stood staring wordlessly at the object in his hands, and Mercury did too.

Wide-eyed, Deviran raised his gaze to his parents, and even from where she stood Mercury could hear the reverence in his voice as he thanked them.

But Mercury had eyes only for the object. No wonder she'd felt it discharge, and no wonder it had felt both strange and familiar. In Deviran's hands lay a glorious, sunshine-gold key, large and strong—and with a handle in the shape of a stylised fish, long, flowing fins curving to make the grip.

A Key. They'd given him a Key. And not just any Key, but *the* Key, *her* Key, the Artefact of Power belonging to *her* city.

A wordless noise of wanting rose in Mercury's throat. Who cared about being dux? She needed that Key.

Keep reading! Head to
<u>amylaurens.com/books/</u>
<u>kaditeos/castle</u>
to buy your copy now!

ABOUT THE AUTHOR

AMY LAURENS is an Australian author of fantasy fiction for all ages. She doesn't usually write tragic or horrific endings, but sometimes they just have to be done.

Amy has also written the award-winning portal-fantasy *Sanctuary* series about Edge, a 13-year-old girl forced to move to a small country town because of witness protection; the humorous fantasy *Kaditeos* series, following newly graduated Evil Overlord Mercury as she attempts to acquire a castle, the forthcoming young adult *Storm Foxes* series about magic and mental health in small town Australia; and a whole host of non-fiction, mostly about dogs and writing.

INKLETS

Collect them all! Released on the 1st and 15th of each month.

INKLET #031
Welcome to Dark Dale
LIANA BROOKS

INKLET #033
When War Came to Town
A Powers Story
AMY LAURENS

INKLET #032
Not Fantasy
AMY LAURENS

INKLET #034
Courting the Winter Prince
LIANA BROOKS

INKLET #035
At the Home of the Winter King
A Storm Foxes Story
AMY LAURENS

INKLET #036
With This Ring
AMY LAURENS

INKLET #037
Venus &
Seven Reasons I Said No
LIANA BROOKS

INKLET #038
OATH KEEPER
AMY LAURENS

INKLET #039
FORGET
A Powers Story
AMY LAURENS

INKLET #040
NOT QUITE Cinderella
LIANA BROOKS

INKLET #041
ONE BAD MAN
AMY LAURENS

DOUBLE ISSUE
INKLET #042
The Claustrophobia Of Loneliness & Adam, Be A Star
AMY LAURENS

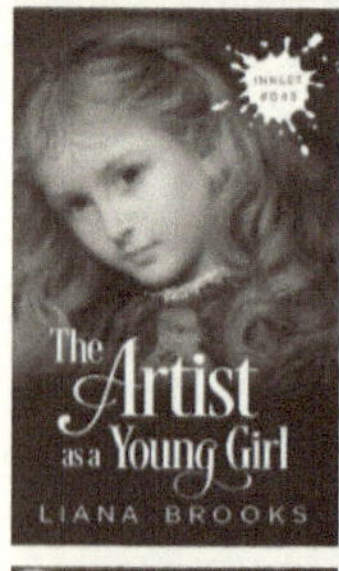

INKLET #043
The Artist as a Young Girl
LIANA BROOKS

INKLET #044
CONFESSIONS
AMY LAURENS

INKLET #045
But For Snow
A Kaitlyn's Story
AMY LAURENS

INKLET #046
The Boy Named NO
LIANA BROOKS

INKLET #047
Anamata
AMY LAURENS

INKLET #048
A Wolf FOR Christmas
AMY LAURENS